For Booth,
my paddling partner in love and life.
And for my friends on Lummi Island,
my shelter in the storm.
—N. L.

For Lizzy,
the best art director
and friend across the seas!
Thank you for your endless
passion, guidance, and support.
—M. C.

SIMON & SCHUSTER BOOKS FOR YOUNG READERS
An imprint of Simon & Schuster Children's Publishing Division
1230 Avenue of the Americas, New York, New York 10020
Text copyright © 2018 by Nina Laden • Illustrations copyright © 2018 by Melissa Castrillon
All rights reserved, including the right of reproduction in whole or in part in any form.
SIMON & SCHUSTER BOOKS FOR YOUNG READERS is a trademark of Simon & Schuster, Inc.
For information about special discounts for bulk purchases, please contact Simon & Schuster
Special Sales at 1-866-506-1949 or business@simonandschuster.com.
The Simon & Schuster Speakers Bureau can bring authors to your live event.
For more information or to book an event, contact the Simon & Schuster Speakers Bureau
at 1-866-248-3049 or visit our website at www.simonspeakers.com.
Book design by Lizzy Bromley • The text for this book was set in Simoncini
Garamond. • The illustrations for this book were rendered in pencil and then
colored digitally. • Manufactured in China • 1117 SCP • First Edition
10 9 8 7 6 5 4 3 2 1 • CIP data for this book is available from the
Library of Congress • ISBN 978-1-5344-0194-5
ISBN 978-1-5344-0195-2 (eBook)

Yellow Kayak

By
Nina Laden

Illustrated by
Melissa Castrillon

A Paula Wiseman Book
Simon & Schuster Books for Young Readers
New York London Toronto Sydney New Delhi

Yellow kayak.
Blue sky.
Paddle swiftly.
Wave good-bye.

Fish jump.
Loons float.

Seals watch.
Little boat.

Shore recedes.
Waves grow.
Adventure begins.
Winds blow.

Yellow kayak.
Gray sky.
Paddle carefully.
Seagulls cry.

Squall starts.
Rain blowing.
Feeling lost.
Keep going.

Wind howls.
Ghostly sounds.
Paddle flies.
Surf pounds.

Yellow kayak.
Lightning streaks.
Thunder roars.
Sea wall leaks.

Rain stops.
Be brave.
Bail boat.
Good save.

Darkness covers.
Fall asleep.
Lapping water.
Dreaming deep.

Yellow kayak.
Sea below.
Squid dance.
Eels glow.

Octopus visits.
Salmon run.
Otters splash.
Having fun.

Shark wanders.
Fish dart.
Seaweed waves.
Clouds part.

Yellow kayak.
Starry sky.
Storm passes.
Fins rise.

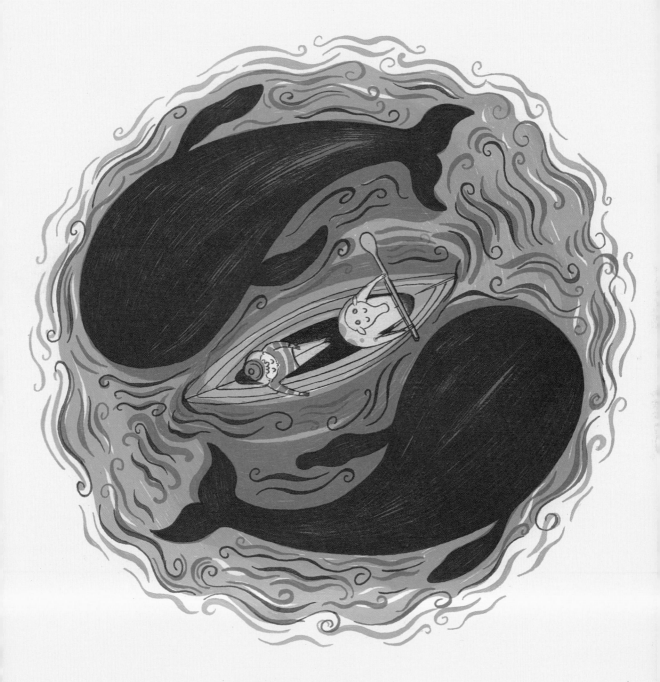

Hulking monsters.
Spray blows.
Circle round.
Danger grows.

Eyes watch,
then understand.
Pushing gently
toward land.

Yellow kayak.
Lighthouse beams.
Welcomes paddler.
Sweet dreams.

Morning dawns.
Rescue boat.
Home comforts.
Happy note.

Orcas dive.
Shunning glory.
Leaving only
this sea story.